A

Wasted

Life

Melvin Sharry

*Our mission is to efficiently provide the world's finest, most comprehensive
book publishing service, enabling every author to experience success.
To find out how to publish your book, your way, and have it available
worldwide, visit us online at www.trafford.com*

Trafford rev. 01/31/2011

 www.trafford.com

North America & international
toll-free: 1 888 232 4444 (USA & Canada)
phone: 250 383 6864 ♦ fax: 812 355 4082

Contents

Acknowledgement

I WOULD LIKE TO DEDICATE this book to several pastor friends that I have lost in death. Throughout these last several years, I always remember their faithful service to the Lord Jesus Christ. How they I am sure at one time or another viewed, a wasted life. But also remembering their dedication and love for the Lord Jesus Christ, they lived their lives to reach lost souls unto Jesus. As I remember each of them individually, they were all great men of God. They are now in the place of the King, and one day I will join them. How I hope that I have been doing and will continue to do, as much as I can, the way they did, to reach others for our glorious Savior. I feel that most people do not appreciate the works that their pastors do, first of all for Jesus, and then for his church, and his people. I remember these great men of God, and the fellowship we had together, they were great friends and I appreciate the ministry of their lives while they were among us. My heart yearns to see them once again.

Melvin Sharry

Summary

THIS IS A STORY, STARTING at the beginning of a young man's life. It reveals his likes and dislikes, even as a child, and in his younger school days. He liked to play, did not like to study. He continued this on through until his high school days. Then there came a sudden change in his ambitions. This continued on through his college days, to the start of his career. There is one constant in this man's life. He cared nothing about the Bible, church or Jesus Christ. He did not get along at all with anyone, who invited him or tried to encourage him in regard to his need for a church family. He was so adamant in his way of doing things, after he was married for three years, and she shared with him, her desire to go to church. He became very cold to her and in about three months. He asked her for divorce. Six months later he was totally living by himself. David did this for the rest of his life, there were little spots of a type of happiness during his life, but they were brief and fleeting. David became a workaholic and seemed to enjoy working hard, either on his job or at home, seven days a week. He did take a lot of pride in the way he kept up his own property. He could have almost lived, as frugal as he was with his money, by the profits he made from selling his fruits and vegetables. One would have to admit, his place always was very nice. He kept his home, very beautiful on the outside and I am sure it was equally beautiful on the inside. His employer was well satisfied with all of his work that he did. In his older years, he received the promotion to office manager. This proved to be almost more work than he could accomplish. In the last phase of his life he became terminally ill with cancer. He had no friends and had no family; his parents had passed away while he was still in high school. As I stated the chaplain of the hospital visited him every day. An everyday tried to share Jesus Christ with him, also trying to pray with him. David would have none of this and he died as he had lived. As I stated there was only nine people at his funeral, two from his work, two from the funeral home, two nurses, the pastor, the chaplain and myself. David had lived a wasted life! It is my prayer that all of us will learn from this man's life, how that we might be able to live a better life.

Melvin Sharry

A

Wasted

Life

Melvin Sharry

1. Beginning of a wasted life!

IN GENERAL ONE WOULD LIKELY think that a life wasted would start at a time or at some point in a person's life. In the case of this life it started when he was an innocent child. He was never given a chance from his parents to have a different life. Then as he was older he had to make his own decisions.

My name is Andrew James and I grew up just down the street from David Wilson. David was a couple of years older than me, but as we grew up we became good friends. We played games together like boys do. I will say that from my earliest memories that David like to play more than anyone else I knew. All boys I knew like to play but at times we had other things we had to do, but David was all about playing. His parents allowed him to be this way.

When school started we all looked forward to recess. When this play time was over, David would continue in the classroom as if he were still at recess, while the rest of the class was trying to do what our teacher was telling us to do. David stayed in more trouble than anyone else in our class. David was the only child of older parents. They both worked all the time and for the most part let David do what ever he wanted to do. I felt that he had the best life, even when we were in the first grade. At my home my parents had big things for me to do, and one of these was my homework. As I look back now I can see the things my parents had me doing really were just petty small things, helping me to learn how life works. My grades at school were pretty good, but David's were terrible. He was a grade ahead of me and he just barely passed. During those elementary years all David wanted to do was play, he did not think that other things were important. On one occasion in class David kept standing up from his desk making all kind of noise, disrupting the class. The teacher told him with a hint of anger, "David sit down and do not get up again until class is over". David did as he was told for about five minuets, he then raised his hand, when the teacher said, yes David, he replied, "I want you to know that on the outside I am setting down, but on the inside I am still standing up". By the time elementary school was over we had started playing little League Baseball, football and basketball, we even started running track. This was right down David's alley; he loved to play any and everything that anyone would come up with. You might even say that David was ball crazy. He did not like to watch sports on television, he wanted to play sports.

My folks had me in Sunday school and Church every Sunday. I enjoyed learning the stories of the Bible. When I would tell David the stories about Jesus, I could tell that David was not very interested. I kept inviting David to go to Sunday school with me; he would always have an excuse. Little did I know at the time the excuses would last through out his entire life? David finally consented to go to Sunday school a couple of Sundays with me. After that he would never go again. His parents did not go to Church, they told David they did not know if there was a God or not. I would continue to invite David to attend Sunday school with me. He continued with his excuses until one day he told me that he did not believe there was a God. By the time we were ready to go into Junior High School, David would not even listen to me when I would try to invite him to go to Church with me. All through Junior High David continued to enjoy nothing but playing. As time went by David had fewer and fewer friends and his grades were very poor and he was barely passing. David and I were now in the same grade; he had failed the Seventh Grade and had to repeat it.

The day had arrived for me and David to start High School. While in Junior High David's grades were just high enough so he could play sports. I will say that David was a very good athlete. Knowing this I along with many others found it hard to believe that now in High School David dropped out of the sports program. It seems what had happened was that David had read a very interesting book; it was so interesting that David started reading nearly all the time. With this new-found interest in books, David's grades started getting better and better. David lost what few friends he had altogether, instead of sports all the time he was now studying all the time. It seemed that he was reading any materials he could get his hands-on. There were others who tried to get David to visit their church with them, his excuses had increased; now he was saying that he did not believe the Bible, and he did not believe there was a God.

His grades had increased until now; he was on the A- honor roll. He was beginning to become nothing but a snob, where other people were concerned. It seemed to others that all he needed was his books, a chair and desk. By the time we had graduated from high school. He had his nose so turned up to the sky, if it were to have rained he would have surely drown. David had become very unlikable. By the time college days had arrived, it seemed he had gotten worse. He enrolled in a college some distance away, he did not attend a school where any of his classmates were attending. While in college, David would become the man he would be for the rest of his life.

2. A young Adult!

BECOMING A YOUNG ADULT IS not easy when the only person you surround yourself with is you. While David was in college he met a young lady by the name of Ann. They started dating on a regular basis. Ann did not know at first, that she was really the only friend that David had. David was doing quite well at this point in his life with his studies, and now he had a young lady in his life. David's major in college was business and management; he felt that he would be able to have a good opportunity for a good job in this particular field. David continued to study and read almost anything he could get his hands on, and as it was earlier in his life. He became absorbed in his own studies, and in the materials that he read, even has he done with sports.

Ann and David began to date more and more as time slipped by. David affection was growing deeper for Ann every day, he began to feel that he had met someone who liked the same things and enjoyed quiet reading time just as he did. Then it happened, Ann asked David if he would like to have children, have a nice house, surrounded by nice neighbors, and they could take their children to Sunday school and church like other families did. At this moment, everything had started to freeze in David's mind. He could not believe what he was hearing, he felt they were so much alike, and now she was talking about children, their children and them going to church. With all these thoughts running through his mind, David lost his composure and began to tell her I do not believe in the Bible or church, I do not believe there is a God! Nothing else was said that night, during the next few days he would only see Ann one-time. The next week David told her that he thought that they believed the same things and wanted to accomplish the same things in their lives. With the difference in spiritual values, and not believing the same things, they would never be able to get along with each other. David told her that he did not want to see her anymore. As David went to bed that night he kept thinking to himself, I know I am right. I did the right thing in breaking up with Ann. Being hard in his heart; David did not ever see Ann again.

David's parents had passed away while he was in high school; they had made provisions for him to get his college education. They left him there home; it was a very nice home, with two bedroom and a spacious living area. The house was a beautiful brick dwelling that stood on five acres of land. The house had an attached garage; on the left side of the house there stood a large shop with an attached small barn. Behind the house was a small grove of fruit trees, behind the shop and barn was a large garden area. These would become very important to David in his life after college. David never gave any thought to living anywhere else; he would live in that same house until the day of his death. For me I would live in about five locations during my life. We would both live in the same town for the rest of our lives. The friendship

David and I should had when we were young, would become just a casual hello as we grew older. Although we were not close friends, I was still able to observe his life as the years went by.

David studied hard, during his college years and made the Dean's list three different times. He became known as a young man with a very bright mind. He would not make friends, therefore he did not have any friends and David did not seem to mind that. Those few college years flew by quiet rapidly, and now it was time for David to graduate from college. He was glad commencement exercises were finally over. He could now get on with the rest of his life. The next thing was to find good employment. In a very short amount of time David found employment with a local company. He moved back from college, into his parent's home, his home. I went by one afternoon and said hello, I asked him how college was and if he was glad to be back home. He said that he was and he told me about his new job and the different things he hoped to accomplish on the home place. He expected the fruit trees to do well and the garden to provide him with a lot of his food needs, thus saving him money at the supermarket. David always had been known for being frugal; most of us said he was just cheap. He explained to me how he was going to make good money and save most of it for his retirement days. He did not seem to leave room for anything or anyone besides himself. I tried again to invite him to come to worship at the church where I went, meet some folks that I thought would be friends that David could have fellowship with. His quick answer was, I told you a long time ago, that I did not believe in that Bible stuff. He said to me, I have my life all mapped out, and I know what I want to accomplish with it. Whatever he wanted to accomplish he did not say, by observation I do not feel that the accomplishment was ever made.

3. Will love change his life?

DAVID ENJOYED HIS PLACE OF employment, and the work he was assigned to do. It did not take long for David to prove that he was very good at the work that was assigned to him. He was happy with his work, and his employer was very satisfied with the job that David was doing. One thing that happened to David, that he was not prepared for, was the day he met Elizabeth. David had accidentally bumped into her cart at the supermarket while shopping. He apologized and she replied, no damage done. David recognized immediately, what an attractive young woman she was. He asked her where she worked; her reply was a clothing store just down the street. It turned out that it was very near the office building where David was employed. He fumbled trying to find the right words, he wanted to ask her out on a date. Finally David asked her if she would like to go out to dinner sometime, her answer came quickly as she said "I would be delighted to go to dinner with you". This would be a romance, for it became that rapidly, and to the casual eye it was not hard to see that this couple deeply cared for each other. They dated seriously over the next year. David made special arrangements at a local restaurant where they enjoyed going, for special evenings. Elizabeth was quite taken with what a beautiful evening they had together, and how beautiful the setting for dinner had been. Just at that moment out from David's pocket he retrieved a small white box that contained a beautiful engagement ring. David was now on one knee, he asked Elizabeth if she would marry him. The look in her face was one of amazement and wonder, like a kid looking through a glass at all the varieties of candy in the window. In an excited voice, she said, certainly I will marry you. They then embraced and begin to talk about when the event could take place and who would be the guest. It seemed as if David's life was taking a turn in the right direction.

It was not long before the wedding date had arrived. And what a beautiful, wonderful day it was. The couple was soon settled in their new home together. He seem to be very happy as they begin to build a life for their future. Elizabeth would soon learn, everyday when David came home from work, he would change from his dress clothes into his work clothes, then head out to work in his small orchard, and in his big garden. This included taking great care of the big yard that surrounded his house. Now this was not just five days a week, David busied himself five days each week at his employment, his evenings and his Saturday, and Sunday, he worked in his shop, in the orchard, garden or in the yard. David could not find enough time to do a thing else. These things and taking care of his job at his office was all David wanted to do. These are the things that they had planned to do with his life; he had not considered what Elizabeth might want to do with her life, as well as their life together.

David was as happy as a dog with a new

bone, working on a job that he enjoyed, going home to take care of his place the way he had always dreamed. One night at supper, Elizabeth asked David if he would like to have children. They had talked about having children once or twice before, David always in a casual way; he would then dismiss the subject. Elizabeth was very serious when she asked David about children, on this particular afternoon. She said that she knew they had spoken of this briefly, a time or two. She said she would love to start a family, and that she would like to start attending church, so they could raise their family in the Lord's house. She realized in recent days, she had not been faithful as a Christian, she also stated that she had an earnest desire to get back in fellowship with Jesus and his family in a local church. She confessed that she really missed not going to church and being a part of a church family. As she was speaking she really was not looking at the discoloration in the face of David. As Elizabeth was sharing from her heart what she had been missing, David was becoming very angry. When she realized that something was wrong with David, she asked if he was okay. He said I am not okay, you did not talk about this when we were dating or any time since they been married. He told Elizabeth that he just assumed that she felt the same way he did. Elizabeth had no idea what David was talking about; this is classic when you leave God out of your life. David told Elizabeth, I do not believe the Bible is true, and I do not believe that there is a God. He slammed his hand against the table, stood up and left the room. David rarely spoke to Elizabeth over the next few weeks. Elizabeth told David that if he did not want to go to church, that would be all right. She continued by saying, I will go to church for myself and maybe one day you will change your mind. David was somewhat in a rage when he said; I am not ever going to church. He told her if that was way she believed the best thing they could do was to get a divorce. Elizabeth was just crushed by what David said. Elizabeth tried a time or two to talk with David, he would only get up and leave the room. For the next three months, they hardly spoke to each other. One Friday when David came home from work Elizabeth was gone, she left a note saying. I love you very much but I cannot live with someone who demands that I deny my faith. About nine months later, the divorce was final, and David was as he had been before, alone. It was not a real hard adjustment for David, for he had lived most of his life by himself. He would once again engulf himself with work on his job, and work on this place.

4. Going it alone!

ONCE MORE DAVID WAS ALL alone. He had rejected the love of Elizabeth, with a closed mind and a closed heart. She asked him about children and caring them to church as a family, which caused David's anger to rise up in him. If only he could have heard the words of Jesus. "Suffer the little children to come unto me and forbid them not for such is the kingdom of God". This would certainly have helped David if he would have just paid attention to what Elizabeth was trying to share with him. He could have known these thing if he would have gone to Sunday School and Church when he was invited as a boy growing up. David was like the man in the Bible that Jesus spoke of, "the fool hath said in his heart, there is no God". This was the way that David was living his life before he met Elizabeth, and continued the same way of life when Elizabeth was gone.

Most people grieve when they lose someone that is real close to them, but it did not seem to bother David at all. I am not sure that David even knew the meaning of love and trust. He went on about his business of being alone and working all the time. If you could have been an observer, you would have never known that David had been married, and that his wife Elizabeth was a very fine woman. Back to work all the time, producing for is employer, then hurrying home to work on his place. As quick as his day was ended at work, David began his work in his garden or something else on his place. His place was very well taken care of; his modest home always had proper maintenance done on it to keep it beautiful. David maintained with equally care his shop and barn. David had a beautiful fence that ran all the way around the perimeter of his five acres. He always kept the fence row, cleaned out which added to the beauty of his home place. Everyone that knew of David called him a workaholic. David seemed to find it easy to be totally absorbed into his work. Work for

David was what entertainment would be for the rest of us. He did not have any friends, where he worked or in the community in which he lived. I feel I would have a hard time being isolated from society, and do nothing but work. It seemed that he hardly had time to eat. He would carry his lunch to work with him and eat at his desk; he would not join his fellow employees in the break room where the rest of them got together for lunch. Different individuals over a period of time would invite him to share lunch with the rest of the employees. David would always decline and his excuse was always the same, I must eat while I work, I do not wish to get behind on my work. There were not a lot of attempts made to include David in social events. He always had an excuse ready of why he could not do, or go; it was because he was so busy. Ever so often someone would invite David to go to church with them. David would always with a snap answer, I do not believe in God.

You can imagine how this would turn individuals away from David with his grouchy attitude. I think there were probably several different individuals with whom David worked that tried at times to be friends with him, but David would just not allow it. David worked seven days a week, five for his employer and two for himself. Sunday was no different to him than any other day of the week. If David would have gone, to Sunday school and church, things might have been different. He could have learned what God said, "six days shall thou labor and do all our work: but the seventh day is the Sabbath of the Lord, the Lord blessed the Sabbath day, and hallowed it". This loner had no time, for anyone in his life, and he denied the existence of God and the salvation that God had provided in his son Jesus Christ. When God said for the whole world, he meant David also. It would have been a marvelous thing, if David would have learned early in life what Isaiah had to say concerning the Lord, "Seek the Lord while he may be found; call upon him while he is near. Let the wicked forsake his way, and the unrighteous man his thoughts, and then return to the Lord, and he (God) will have mercy on him".

David grew a lot of vegetables and fruits, and put up as much as he needed for himself. Then he would sell the rest to anyone who wanted to buy fresh fruits and vegetables. He made a good profit every year, from the things he grew on his own property. I remember on one occasion, passing by David's home, he was working in the yard. I stopped to talk with him, he was friendly enough, but he did remind me that he was very busy. I asked him how he felt working all the time and not having any friends. His response was that it was okay with him, for he had so much work to do and was so busy that he did not notice that there were no people around. The work must be done, he said it had to be done and he was certain, no one was going to do the work for him. He also told me that I ought to try it, I might find it very rewarding being busy all the time. I think I will be busy, and take care of everything that needs to be cared for. I also feel that there are many things in this life that God intended for us to enjoy and be a part of. David was going through the motions of living, but he was missing what living is all about. Somewhere at some point in his life he had listened to the whispers of Satan who told him that there was no God and the Bible is not true. Very, very sad when an individual gets wound up, tied up and bound up in the lies of Satan and misses what life really is all about? It is a sad type of existence the way David was living, but God did give to each individual the right to choose how to live and what to believe in. Each individual should at least have an open mind, but it was more evident every day that David's mind was totally closed, regarding things that were for is own well-being. I like myself; but I do not like myself enough just to have myself and no one else for company. I feel that this would be a very bitter, as well as difficult way to approach or to live life. This is the way that David chose to live his life; I feel that David was extremely miserable. He would just not allow anyone to see into his heart. Day by day, he was just becoming more miserable and his heart was overflowing with grief. To my knowledge, I don't think David ever spoke of Elizabeth, at least not in public. He had decided to go it alone, spend all of his time working either on his job or on his place.

5. I am just worn out!

I DO NOT BELIEVE THAT David ever thought that he would get to the place where he would just get much too tired. His day by day, work ethics began to be very trying. He began to notice that he could not work as long each day as he was used to doing. When he would come home from work and start working on his place, he used to work till almost time to go to bed. He worked outside until it started getting dark, then he would go into his shop and work until it was time to get ready for bed. Now each evening, as it would grow close to darkness, he was ready to go in the house and get in his recliner, with something cool to drink, and rest for he was worn out.

He was like those in the Bible that Jesus talked about, "and they with one consent, began to make excuse, I bought a piece of ground, I have bought some oxen, I am too busy" (ms). If David would have learned this type of behavior when he was young, it might have changed his life. He might not have fell victim to this kind of behavior himself. He could have learned, "enter you into the rest of the Lord Jesus Christ". The sadness is that David never learned the things from God that would have been help to him in order to have a more satisfying life. I have done work on some building, houses, shops and various things; I did much of his work by myself. But much of the work I had to have some help. You understand what I am talking about. If you tried to put in place a 2"x6"x12 ft., and 8 foot from the floor. You need help; you need someone to hold the other end in place while you attach the end that you are working on. To me, life is a lot like that. There are times we can do certain things by ourselves and other times, we need someone to help us. David tried to do everything himself, and living unto himself is like trying to hang the timber I was talking about by yourself. You will always struggle, it is not impossible to do everything yourself, it is almost impossible to place that timber by yourself. I am just expressing that sometimes it make sense to have some help. I feel that David did a lot of struggling as he was going it alone. He had no one to help him; he lived his life in isolation from society. I can only imagine the kind of loneliness that must have been in David's life. I doubt seriously if David would ever admit that he was lonesome. Or that he desired companionship and friendship in his life. I said he would not admit it, not that he did not feel lonesome. By observation, one could see that he was wrapped up in his work, be it on the job or at home. Discussions and arguments do not have to be of the hurtful kind. All of us, except for David at least, have had these experiences in our lives. Which makes me wonder if David ever had an argument or discussion with himself, in order just to have someone to talk with? David had a great education, and he had learned how to farm and did a great job for his employer. One would think that with all that knowledge he would have been desirous to have some friends in his life. David did not just say he was busy, by observation anyone could tell that he was constantly working (he was busy). And to a lot of individual's amazement he seemed totally content living in his isolation from the world. Young kids would walk by his place poking fun at him. They would laugh and talk and point at him as he worked on his place, and tell each other there is the old hermit or that is where the old hermit lives. David would always wave at people as they came by his place and they would usually wave back. This was about the extent of David's dealing with society. I remember as a boy visiting my grandparent's who lived deep in the country. At night I would hear the howling of a wolf. My grandfather would say that the howling of the wolf was the loneliest sound that he had ever heard. To me, it did sound very lonely. I wonder if David ever heard the howling of a wolf. If he did, did it sound lonely to him? David is not a wolf, but the way he was living his life seemed to have the same type of loneliness like the sound of a wild wolf. David seemed to be very content, it seemed so to those that observed his life. How could anyone be content in such isolation.

6. Some effort at life!

SOME THINGS WERE ABOUT TO happen in David life that would for the time seem to change his life. His employer, had also observed David's isolation from people, and at the same time, he was appreciating the work he did for his company. Mr. Henderson, David's employer, was making plans on how David, could be even more valuable to his company. He also knew that he needed to get David to realize how important it was to mix with other people. Mr. Henderson had a promotion in mind for David, and this would include a closer involvement with other employees. Mr. Henderson after much talking convinced David to become a part of the Lions Club. By making this move, David would become more involved with people. He would deal with whatever program the Lions Club had going on at the time. Believe it or not, David became really involved with the program and people of this club. They were constantly involved in some kind of social activity, and David was enjoying the activities.

David, at one of the clubs events, met a nice woman his own age. It seemed like that things were going to change in David's life. Diane was an attractive woman for her age and pleasant in her manners. Quite often, David would invite her out to dinner and a movie. It seemed they were becoming good friends. David was doing his best to follow his employer's suggestion concerning other employees. It seemed to the outside observer that David was happier with a smile on his face. He also had a friendlier attitude, and a much more cordial approach with others. This new life continued on for several months. David even stopped some of the work that he was doing on his place, to make room for other things that were taking place in his life.

Could it be possible that after all these years that David would cease to be the workaholic he had been most of his life. It seemed that we were seeing a new David. One Saturday afternoon he invited Diane to his place, he showed her his home, workshop and barn. They spent a great deal of time walking around and talking, while he was showing her his orchard and his garden. He shared with her, how much time and work that it took in caring for his place. David worked with care to keep the trees in his orchard in good condition. He shared how he worked his garden for best production, how much labor was needed in keeping his fences cleared of vines and weeds. That same evening, he took Diane to their favorite restaurant for evening dinner. They seem to enjoy each other's company, and they had a great time that day.

Would this seemingly new day be permanent, or was it just for a brief time. As it always had been, it was about to happen again. One evening while he and Diane were eating at the restaurant, the old lightning would strike again. Diane was asking him about his life and family. David with great manners shared with her, how he lost his parents while he was still in high school. He quickly added that he had no other family as for as he knew. As they continued in conversation, Diane asked him what church he attended. The nice manners came to an end, as David made his reply. Diane, I want you to understand that I do not believe that there is a God; I think the Bible is just another book, I do not believe in heaven or hell or in this man they call Jesus Christ. Diane was shocked; because she felt like in her own heart, that she knew David better than what she did. After this brief conversation the meal wound up rather suddenly. David carried Diane back to her home, and told her, I don't think we ought to see each other anymore.

In the days that followed, David quit going to the club meetings. He still tried to maintain a type of friendliness to the other employees. Once again, David plunged himself into his work, both on the job and at home. He told himself that he had a lot of catching up to do, because he allowed himself to be taken in by these other activities. True to form David returned to the same type of person he had always been. It is a shame that David never gave himself the opportunity to learn from the Bible, if he would have done this. It would have changed his life. He always said that he was working at his business or working on his place. Maybe one day I will have time for some of these others things that people talk about. The Bible states, "When they have heard, they go forth, and are choked with cares and pleasures of this life". Luke said that, and many other things that could have help David if he would have only paid attention to those who had invited him to church, to worship God and his son Jesus Christ. David has once again returned to a lonely miserable life.

7. Bible accounts of a wasted life!

WE LOOK FOR BRIEF TIME at Jehoram King of Judah. This particular man is a great example of a wasted life. I use the word wasted life in the context of a life that is lived to oneself. Perhaps this is more of a wasted life because of the harm and damage he does to other persons, even to the damage of a nation. Jehoram came to the throne of Judah at the age of 32. He was the son of Jehoshaphat, king of Judah, "which did that which was right in the eyes of the Lord". "When he died he was buried with his fathers in the city of David". This is the account that the book of Chronicles gives us concerning a great man. His son would become King; he would be just the opposite of his father, and because of his evil ways. He would only be

King for eight years. He started off by doing the most horrible thing that a man could do. He killed all his brothers. So they would not be a threat to his throne or his rule.

The next thing that Jehoram did was getting married. On the hearing of such a statement one might ask, what is wrong with getting married? It's not getting married, that was wrong; it was the type of person that he married. The Bible tells us that her mother was a wicked woman, more than any other woman, who had lived, her name was Jezebel. That being said, I would say, the runner-up to Jezebel was Athaliah the daughter of Ahab and Jezebel. Ahab was King of Israel, and did that which was evil in the site of the Lord. Seeing who it was that he married, he being evil and marrying evil, you can imagine the kind of evil (evil + evil = total evil)! Evil they would spread like a disease over the nation of Judah; he followed in the steps of Ahab and the King's of Israel. The Bible states that he caused the inhabitants of Jerusalem to commit fornication. He was not only evil in himself, but led others into evil.

The prophet Elijah knowing of the evil that

Jehoram had committed, wrote him a letter. In this letter, Elijah states God's message; "because thou has caused my people to sin, and caused them to commit whoredoms as Israel has done, acting in the same manner as Ahab of Israel. With a great plague, the Lord will smite thy people, and thy children, and thy wives, and all thy goods. And thou shall have great sickness and disease of thy bowels and all thy bowels will fall out, by reason of thy sickness on a day by day basis" ms. What an indictment this was against this King. One would think this would draw him to his knees seeking God's forgiveness; his heart was set to live evil and do evil. What a shame for man to make a decision as Jehoram made. The Ethiopians and the Arabians were stirred up against Judah, and came against her, and killed all of his sons except Jehoahaz his youngest. "So the Lord smote his bowels with an incurable disease. After two years, by reason of this disease he died a horrible death" ms. "The nation of Judah made no burning for him, as they had done for his father; they buried him in the city of David, but not in the sepulcher of the King's" ms. He was 32 years old when he became king, and he ruled for eight years, and the Bible states. "He died without being desired" ms. This tells me that this was a man who lives for 40 years, and his life was wasted. It is an awful thing to live a life, and abuse that life, as well as everyone around you. Murdering your brothers, leading your nation to commit gross sins against God, and he married a woman, you could not have found one more wicked than Athaliah was. If we were to give his life, a title it would have to be, "Forty wasted years".

If David would have gone to Sunday school and church, and read such a story as this, perhaps it would have changed his life. What I see as I look into David's life is a wasted life, and very poor as God is concerned. A life that could have been redeemed, but he had blocked God completely out of his mind and heart; he would not read the Bible that was shared with him. Telling him of God's gift of salvation, which he could have in the Lord Jesus Christ? It is a pity that David was so busy that he did not take time to look into the things that pertained to his own peace.

8. The management position!

THE DAY ARRIVED WHEN DAVID received what he thought was great news. Mr. Henderson came into the office, where David was working and told him he wanted to talk with them. He told David that he had been observing him through the years he had been his employee and was well pleased with his work ethics, and his productivity. I need someone like you in this company to keep the business growing and producing to the best of its ability. I want you to become the office manager, and director of productivity. I believe that you can help keep this company growing and making a good profit in the days ahead. He also told David that there would be a substantial increase in salary in this new position. He asked David if he needed time to think it over, David's reply was that he would give him an answer the following day. David did not get much work done around his place that afternoon. He was much too excited about the new promotion that was being offered to him. After all these years, David felt that his hard work and industrious behavior had finally paid off.

As David was preparing to go to work, he was still excited about his new job, and he kept telling himself, things will be different now. When he arrived at work, Mr. Henderson showed him to his new office. It was quite a bit bigger than his old office, and quite a bit nicer. He had a great big desk and a very comfortable office chair. Before that day was over his big new desk was stacked full of folders filled with work that needed be done. He soon learned that this job was more about work production than being a manager over other employees. He did not shrink from the task that was before him. David did, as he always had done, engulf himself at being busy taking care of all the work that was placed before him. If anyone would have suggested faith in God, David would have said I am to busy to worry about God or anything else. I am responsible to keep this company growing and making a profit. David soon found out that he was not as young as he used to be, and the work took longer to accomplish, and it was much more difficult. He also found out, at his age. He was too tired to work on his place as he had always done, when he came home from his job. If David could have heard what God said, "Thou fool this night thy soul shall be required of thee, then who will own your nice place" (ms).

David always had been a handsome fellow with a nice-looking head of hair. Now when David looked in the mirror, his face sagging, and he was totally bald. Years of hard work were beginning to not only take a toll on him. But he was just becoming a very grouchy old man. He found that he could not get along with the others who were employed to work with him. He had to be quite harsh with them, keeping them busy for the sake of productivity. One thing about David, he did not ask his employees to do what he himself was not already doing. We have to get this work done, and he did is part to see that it was done. David felt in the beginning, with this new promotion that things would be easier, but in fact, they become much more difficult as well as harder to accomplish. He found himself being worn out before lunch time. He still had over a half a day before quitting time, he would push himself all day to see that the work got done. David was beginning to wonder why his energy was all used up before noon everyday. He always enjoyed good health, and a strong body. He contributed his lack of energy to his rigid work habits that he had done all his life. He also figured that because of his work habits, and always being busy, was the reason for his good health. As the days dragged on David Seemed to be getting weaker and weaker not knowing that he had a disease.

David had rarely seen a doctor, during his life because of his good health. He decided that it was time for him to make appointment with the doctor and asked him why he was getting weaker and weaker, and it was becoming almost impossible to get his work done. He asked some of the other employees if they could recommend a good doctor. Many doctors were recommended. One doctor's name came up more than the others. So David decided to get an appointment with this doctor and go in for an examination. The day soon arrived for David's appointment at the doctor's clinic. As David set in the waiting room, his mind was in a whirl in regard to what the doctor might tell him. In ones mind, one can imagine almost anything, and that was what was going on in David's mind as he waited for his name to be called. After what seemed a long time a nurse finally called his name, and took him to an examination room, and was told the doctor would be in to see him in a few minutes.

9. Too late for God!

As David set waiting for the doctor to come into the room. He had no idea that he was about to be given a new excuse. That would be, I am much too sick, and much too old to think about God now. Unknown to David, the news he was about to receive would be almost more than anyone could bear. Finally the doctor came into the room; he introduced himself to David and asks him exactly what was bothering him. David's shared with him the way he felt and the way is energy level and fallen off. The doctor, listen to what David had to say, patiently taking notes of each thing that David shared. The doctor then told him that they needed to run several tests, in order to find out what was going on in David's body.

The doctor suggested, because of the number of tests that need to be run that David would need to be admitted to the local hospital. This gave David quiet a shock; he thought it would just be something simple that he could take a pill for. Then things would be all right and he could return to work. But the doctor said he had to enter the hospital for a whole multitude of test.

David took leave from work and went to the local hospital and was admitted. It would take several days for all the tests to be run. After several days had gone by the doctor entered his room and told David that the tests were conclusive. He said he had also consulted with other physicians. Then came the bad news, the doctor told David that he had leukemia (a type of blood cancer). The doctor shared with David, the different treatments, and the treatment should begin as soon as possible. The treatments were started the next day, and as they continued. David became weaker and weaker as the days went by.

One morning, after David had been taking treatments for quite a while, Mr. Henderson his employer entered his room. Mr. Henderson stay was brief, and this is what he told David. David, you have been a good employee for these many years, but because of your health problems and your age. I will have to replace you with someone else. You have always done a good job, and I appreciate that. I hope thing go well with you, goodbye. David's mind was in a whirl he had been employed at this place of business all his working life. Nothing of retirement, not even a small gift of appreciation for all that he had done. He thought surely, when his working days were over, (he did not contemplate that they would end due to illness), there would be some kind of gift of appreciation for all his years of labor. Needless to say he was very disappointed.

David's disease had really taken its toll on his body and his mind as well. He was so sick and now he felt very old. David had no one to come to see him, no friends and no family. If he only would have accepted some of those invitations to worship God and come to know the Lord Jesus Christ, he would have had a very large church family. That would have been very concerned for the condition that he was in. The church has responsibility to love and care for folks even though they do not know them, but David had so isolated himself and had withdrawn from society, that no one knew who he was.

While David was in the hospital, the hospital Chaplain came to see him everyday. He tried to talk to him about his soul, tried to read the Bible, and also tried to pray with him. David would just wave one hand and say I am too old, too sick to think about God or anything else. Each day I am a little weaker than I was yesterday, David would say. Every day the Chaplain would come by his room and stand by his bedside and pray silently for him. David would never consent for him to read the Bible or to talk with him about heaven and hell or receiving Jesus Christ as his Savior. I am to sick, too tired; I am a very old man. I thought that I would get well and return to my home and be able to work in my yard and in my garden. And at times I would like work in my workshop. Then came the day the doctor came by and told him that he had only two or three more days to live. You would think that being told, this kind of news would open one's heart to the word of God. The Chaplain came by, at least three times a day, sometimes more, until David passed away. He would never allow the Bible be read or prayers to be said. The

Chaplain and the nurses all prayed for David every day, not so much for his health but for his soul. I have heard many times, and I am sure that is true, that most people die as they have lived. In the case of David, this was certainly true. When I heard of David situation, and I heard how he responded to the Chaplain who was only trying to help him during these very difficult days. I thought to myself, David, you could have done anything in your life that you desired for good. But by your own choosing you rejected what would have been the best thing for you in life. You lived, a wasted life. David passed from this life, a few hours later, like the king of Judah, "he died without being desired".

10. Facing God!

LIFE IS OVER FOR DAVID and nothing on this earth matters any more, all that is left for David is a funeral. David's funeral was a very sad occasion. People were not concerned about his death, they did not know him. It would be a sad situation for there would be no one present at his funeral. When I heard of his death, I begin to wonder how many people might be present. After thinking about it for a few minutes I decided that I would attend his funeral service. Seeing it for myself is the reason I know it was a sad situation. The funeral personnel (two of them), myself, one nurse and the Chaplain from the hospital and two people that worked for the same employer he had worked for his whole life, were all that were in attendance. David had lots of money in the bank; you could almost say he was a rich man. David was very poor in spirit, this by his own choosing. I did not mean to forget, but a local pastor and agreed to do the service, which made a total of eight people at a funeral. It was a very brief service; we then adjourned to the cemetery. He was buried in the southwest corner of the local cemetery. And that was a brief service as well, myself ,the pastor, the Chaplain, the two general employees and the two that dug the grave, were standing off at some distance. Maybe for the first time I realize what the Bible meant when it said "he died without being desired".

After living 72 years, I know that to be true for on the small stone was written is name, the day he was born and the day he died. After his rejection at 72 years, the one in whom David did not believe, he is now face-to-face with. I do not know if David even believed he had a soul, but he knows it now. He understands the soul, his soul is dead, but it will always exist, he will give account of himself, unto God. I know from my study of God's word that David now wishes he would have accepted those many invitations he had received during life, but it is too late now. He would be like children in games wanting a (do over), that is another chance. A few days later, after the funeral I went out to the cemetery and I really do not know why, but I did. I walked slowly, all over the cemetery, looked at all the stones and markers and reading what they had to say. After quite some time, I wound up in the southwest corner of the cemetery, where David's body was placed. I looked on the small head stone, and my mind carried me back to the days when David and I were boys, thinking of those childhood memories, never dreaming that David would live a wasted life on this earth.

I HAVE NO IDEA WHAT will become of David's property all the money in the bank. He never felt the need to make a will, and having no family, his property and his money are just lying there, waiting I suppose for the state to take care of them. If David could come back from the grave he would certainly tell people how important it is to believe in God, and read his word, receive his gift of salvation in the Lord Jesus Christ. I drove by David's place a few days ago and it is overgrown with grass, weeds, vines, his Orchard is in much need of care, his fence rows are all grown up with grass and weeds, and his house and barn need paint and repair. I know in my heart. I should have tried harder and witnessed the love of God, with David; it might not have changed any thing. As Christians we need to go the extra mile to help people find their way to the Cross of Jesus. One must come to the cross of Jesus, then accept him as your Savior. I should have tried harder to reach David for God, just as you need to try harder to reach people that you know for God. For as it was with David so will it be with us, all of us will have to give an account of the things that we have done in this life, whether it be good or bad. Remember what God's word says, "it is appointed unto man once to die, then the judgment". What good are we trying to do with our lives each day that will honor and glorify our Lord and Savior Jesus Christ? The Bible tells us, "He that wins souls is wise". As I walked through the cemetery, where David is buried I saw an inscription that is very true, "as you are now, so once was I, as I am now, one day you shall be". Time is rolling past us rapidly; it is time that we understand, "all the good that I can do, I must do it now. For you see, I will never pass this way again".

11. This was your life!

A PREVIEW OF YOUR LIFE in its entirety would have to begin when you were a small baby. God would reveal in a panoramic view, all the things that you ever did, and that means, if they were good or if they were bad. We live our lives to one degree or another, the way we want to live them. We did a lots of good in our lives, we also did some things were not so good. We have done things we wish we could forget about, and we certainly wish God would forget about them. That's not going to happen; we shall give an account of ourselves to God, for the good, for the bad. Praise God He will forgive us of our sins, but we will still have to give an account of our lives unto him. There are a lot of people who wish that the good they have done would outweigh the bad, they have done. Unfortunately, that is not the way it works. One enters into heaven through his or her relationship with the Lord Jesus Christ. If one has not accepted the Lord Jesus Christ as their personal savior. They certainly will not enter the joy of heaven, but spend eternity in the endless leagues of night, with all manner of terror. After our life on earth is over, we will be placed in a grave until the rapture of the church, "at the trumpet sound we shall rise to meet the Lord in the air, so shall we ever be with the Lord" ms. If you die not knowing the Lord Jesus Christ as your Savior, you also will be placed in the grave. And you will remain in the grave until the time of the white throne judgment of God. Then you will be summoned from the grave to appear before God's white throne judgment. He will declare unto you that he never knew you and you shall be cast into the Lake of fire, where the beast and false prophets are.

So we take a look at, this is your life. Things that you have forgotten about, things you have seen, things you have talked about, times you were in church. God will reveal these things to you in a panoramic fashion. So you can see why you are being judged very clearly. Things like hypocrisy, backbiter, unmerciful, pride, envy, disobedient to parents , deceit, whisper, lies, warmongers, theft, hater of God, false accuser, these and many others will be revealed to you in this panoramic view of your life. You might say, why did not someone tell me, they did, through God's Word, singing, things being said around you, you were being warned, but you did not listen. That is the way it was in David's life. You might say look there, see I was in church, but where you listening with your heart to what the preacher was saying. When the preacher told you how to be saved, did you listen, or did you say, I could care less. Perhaps what he was saying was to close to your heart and you just got up and left. Now you hear the summons to appear before God. God asked the angel to open the book of life to see if your name is recorded their. He looks more than one time, he wants to be sure. Then he says, Lord. His name does not appear in this precious book. And immediately God will say, "depart from me, ye cursed, into everlasting fire, prepared for the devil and his angels". This is exactly what the Book of Revelations tells us is going to happen. If you could only see the darkness of that horrible place and that lake of fire burning, rolling, churning with the multiplied millions that are cast there in, it ought to get your attention. If you do not know Jesus, you will be among them. It would certainly be wise, if you gave care to your soul. I'm not sure I know what you're talking about. I'm talking about turning from your sins. This is called repentance, asking Jesus to forgive you for all your sins and invite him into your heart, receiving him as Lord and Savior of your life. He will then write your name in his book, if your name is not in his book. You have never received Christ as your Savior. If you reject him as your Savior, as David did, as sure as there is day and night you will spend eternity in something worse than hell, that burning lake of fire.

This can be your life, and you hear the preacher speak of repent and receive Christ. And you will become a new creature. You might say, I believe the Bible, but what must I do to be saved. You must be born again, even as you are born on this earth, you must be born from heaven. And the only way you can be born from heaven is by receiving Jesus Christ into your life, confessing that you are a sinner and asking the Lord Jesus to be your savior. Then you will have many things in your life that are good, praying, witnessing, singing, giving, sharing Bible stories with your children or other children, sharing the Word of God, thanking God for your food when you sit down to eat, hospital visitation, caring for the sick, and the elderly, wonderful times of great fellowship with other believers, every opportunity, worshiping and praising God. There will be a time, just as there was a time for the lost man, the death Angel will come for you, at that moment, and you will know you are headed for that heavenly home. The sweetest words that you ever heard will be spoken, "well done, thou good and faithful servant----enter thou into the joy of the Lord". The Bible tells us, "but as it is written, eye has not seen, nor ear heard, neither have entered into the heart of man, the things which God had prepared for them that love him". This is a quote from First Corinthians 2:9, and you can Bank on it.

David wasted his life; he never entertained thoughts concerning God and his Word through his church. He never let anyone talk to him about Jesus Christ. David died as he had lived. The choice was always his, and I certainly believe he made the wrong choice. From time to time in his life, heaven and hell were presented to him. When we were children I invited David to church, many other children did so as well. The Sunday School Teacher told David of Gods Love. His girlfriends did as well as His wife, she told him. His co-workers invited him. The Chaplain at his bed side tried many times to share with him. He must of heard of Easter and Christmas with their beautiful music about the Lord Jesus Christ. The opportunity comes from many sources and directions. The choice was his to make, just as the choice is yours to make. It is my earnest prayer that you make the right choice. Would you, no matter where you are, in your home, car, place of work, wherever you may be, right now bow your head and open your heart and pray inviting the Lord Jesus Christ into your heart? You must ask him to forgive you of your sins and invite him to live in your heart and be your Lord and Savior. When you have done this you need to find a local church, where you can become a member and become involved in the ministry of your Savior Jesus Christ. The most important decision you or anyone else can make is given to us from the book of Acts 16:31, "believe on the Lord

Jesus Christ and thou shall be saved, and thy
house".

***DO NOT LIVE A WASTED LIFE! ***

Epilogue

IN THIS SECTION OF THE book the idea is to convey a summary of what happened to the characters in the book. I would certainly like to say that everything turned out real well for the main character but that is not the case. We followed him from the time of his youth until he was dying of leukemia in the hospital. Throughout all his years he never had time, was not interested, actually said he did not believe in God, or his word, or his son, or his church. We see time and again where he had opportunity for a good life but he would not take advantage of the opportunities that were given to him. One true fact, no matter how much you share with someone else about what Christ can do for them; Christ can do nothing if they do not believe. Our precious Savior is not going to force anyone to go to heaven that choice is given to each individual that lives on this earth; it's up to them to make the right decision.

While David was very sick in the hospital the chaplain came every day and tried to tell him of God's love, tried to read God's word to him and tried to pray with him. All the things were done to no avail. The main character had closed his heart from the love of God. We express the scene we saw at the cemetery, it only leaves an empty place in one's heart. There were no flowers, he had no friends to bring flowers, and no one cared enough to give flowers. Only a small marble headstone with his date of birth and the day of his death, that is all there was. We then took a step further to look at the time that David would see God in the Day of Judgment. We viewed a mental picture of him being cast in the like of fire; it was not a very pleasant picture. It is our earnest desire that each of us live in such a way as to help those who are living (A Wasted Life), we may be their only means of hearing of Gods wonderful salvation in his Son, The Lord Jesus Christ.

Yours in Christ

Melvin Sharry

Is

God

Serious

"Let us hear the conclusion of the whole matter: Fear God, and keep his COMMANDMENTS: for this is the whole duty of man". Ecclesiastes 12:13

Melvin Sharry

Contents

Acknowledgment

I DEDICATE THIS BOOK TO my father, the Rev. Walter Sharry for the many years of service that he has given in service to our Lord and Savior Jesus Christ. Being the pastor of a church and preaching the Gospel of Jesus Christ for 60 years. Always doing his best to honor his Savior and sharing his Savior with those who were lost. Not many men have the opportunity for this length of preaching the word of God. I am thankful for the work accomplished and ministry performed. He has been a help to many as well as a help to me. I am thankful for his life, things he achieved and dreams fulfilled. He understands that we will pass this way once, all the good we can do we must do it as we travel through life, for we will never pass this way again. There is no way for us to measure how his ministry will affect eternity. A lot of people have been saved as a result of his life. I thank my Lord and Savior Jesus Christ, for his life that my Lord has given him to live.

Melvin Sharry

Preface

THIS BOOK IS A SHORT book, but it is a very important book to us in this nation as well as it is to those in the rest of the world. God is very serious about his Ten Commandments and we must get very serious about them as well. We have left them out of our lives as well as our communities and our nation. I am fearful that in very many cases, we have left them out of our churches. It is time for us to evaluate how these laws of God are part of our lives. God did his part as he wrote with his own finger these laws on the tablets of stone. Moses brought them down the mountain to give them to the rest of mankind forever. It is up to us whether or not we are going to keep his Commandments for guidance and direction as we live here on this earth. We must and I implore you to take serious, what God has given to us. Let no man or groups of men ever deprive you of what God is given you to direct your life and give you guidance in your daily life.

Melvin Sharry

1. Is God Serious!

IN ORDER FOR US TO understand how serious God is about his laws that he has given us and has told us that we should keep his commandments. I think a good look at what Jesus had to say along with the apostles might give us a better understanding of how important these laws really are. The Bible tells us as is recorded in John's Gospel "he that hath my commandments, and keeps them, he it is that love's me: and he that loves me shall be loved of my father, and I will love him, and will manifest myself to him". This verse makes it pretty plain how Jesus felt about the Commandments. Jesus then reverses the statement, and puts the load of his statement on our shoulders. In the book of

John, the apostle writes "he that said, I know him, and keep not his commandments, is a liar, and the truth is not in him". The apostle is telling us a great value concerning God's Ten Commandments. Those individuals who make a pretense of the law, his life is like a mirror and will reflect the truth of what he says. Simply if you say you know Jesus and keep not his commandments (seriously trying to keep them) that you are a liar and the truth is just not there.

There was a rich man that came to Jesus and asked him a question. A question that a lot of us would like to know the answer to, the question concerning eternal life. Which is the greatest commandment, are they all equal? I feel that in essence they are all equal, remember now Jesus is the authority in any thing that is mentioned, so the rich man asked what is the greatest commandment. "Jesus said unto him, thou shall love the Lord thy God with all our heart and with all thy Soul, and with thy entire mind. This is the first and great commandment. And the second is like unto it, thou shall love thy neighbor as thyself. On these two commandments hang all the law and the prophets".

Do the Commandments have anything to do with salvation? In a certain sense they do not, but in a clear light they have everything to do with salvation. They give us a clear understanding of what salvation is to be in the eyes of God. This brings up another quotation from the word of God taken from the Gospel of Mark. "There came one running to him, and kneeled to him, and asked him, good Master, what shall I do that I may have eternal life? And Jesus said to him, why call me good? There is none good but one, that is, God. You know the Commandments, do not commit adultery, do not kill, do not steal, do not bear false witness, defraud not, honor thy father and thy mother. He answered and said unto him, Master, all these things have I observed from my youth. Then Jesus beholding him loved him, one thing you lack: go thy way, sell whatsoever thou hast, and give it to the poor, and thou shall have treasures in heaven: take up thy cross, and follow me. And he was sad at the saying, and went away grieved: for he had great possessions". There are some that almost understand the Ten Commandments. They allow these laws of God to miss their hearts and they allow other things to keep them from obeying what is in their best interest. When man does not want to obey God he tries to figure out someway to indulge himself that the laws of God are not that important.

And still as we search the Scriptures we come to passages that reads just a little bit differently which causes us to some extent to rearrange what we have already said. Mark's Gospel also states "which is the first commandment of all? Jesus answered him, first of all the commandments is, hear oh Israel; the Lord our God is one Lord. Thou shall love the Lord thy God with all thy heart, with all thy soul, with thy entire mind, and with all thy strength, this is the first commandment". There are people who try to make everything fit them rather than them fit with obedience to the laws of God. You will never find peace when you try to disallow what God's word has said. So according to Jesus the Ten Commandments are very important of which he says, first you must love God supremely. When you love God supremely you will want to obey him and do his will with your life. You will become faithful in his church, doing your best to follow the leadership of his

Holy Spirit. It might be that you would make a good teacher, sing in the choir, take up the offering, always be involved in reaching out to others that they might find their way to salvation, remember, your pastor cannot do it by himself. Have an active prayer life and Bible study every day and always be ready to help in the church anyway you possibly can. As you keep the Ten Commandments they will be strength to you as you travel through this life. These laws of God are for all of us, to aid us as we serve our Savior, enabling us to help our family, friends and neighbors. The Law of God will bring out the very best in our lives, if we do our best to obey them.

2. The Ten Commandments:

1. "Thou shall have no other gods before me".

2. "Thou shall not make any graven images".

3. "Thou shall not take the name of the Lord thy God in vain".

4. "Remember the Sabbath day and keep it holy".

5. "Honor thy father and thy mother".

6. "Thou shall not kill".

7. "Thou shall not commit adultery".

8. "Thou shall not steal".

9. "Thou shall not bear false witness against thy neighbor".

10. "Thou shall not covet anything that is thy neighbor".

3. The Value of Gods Laws!

I WANT TO WRITE A few lines in regard to our subject, the Ten Commandments. These are the standard by which all the world measures the fall of Saints, especially the community of Christians. I cannot emphasize enough how we as Christians do not have enough compassion and forgiveness in our hearts toward our fellow man. I was listening to the radio as I was traveling down the highway; the announcer began to share a survey by a certain group that had been taken recently. The survey was taken from a cross section of Christians of all denominations. The analysis of the survey I already knew from experiences that I had experienced in my life. The answer to the survey was a sad indictment against

Christians; this is not a survey of everyone, rather a survey of quote, unquote of Christians. The answer they gave to the survey, of all the people in our country. Christians are the most unforgiving, unconcerned, uncaring, lack of compassion, more than any other group that was surveyed. These are the things we ought to be rated the highest in, certainly not at the very bottom of the survey. We must not like sin in other people's lives but we certainly ought to be the first to forgive them when they stumble and fall. The Christian acts like he or she wants to help, but they have their hand turn downward when they give the impression that they are going to help you up. When you help someone that has fallen, when you reach out your hand it must be turned upward, so that you will be able to help them up. For this reason I will write a few lines in regard to sin and forgiveness. Sin that is of the flesh is the sin that people want to talk about the most. There is a lot more to the Ten Commandments than just one. The first one is "thou shall not have any other gods before me". These other gods are not the same thing to them, as adultery would be. I will repeat over and over again, if the Ten Commandments are co-equal in the eyes of God should we not do our best to keep them all. I realize that there are some sins that affect individuals as well as families to their hurt more than others. I think the question arises how God looks upon, The Ten Commandments he gave to Moses. Jesus said "if you have broken one of the least of these commandments you are guilty of all", is he trying to tell us how God looks upon all his commands. I am not trying to make an excuse for the sins that cause any person to fall; I am trying to say that any Saint can fall also, by breaking any one of these commandments. I do not feel that the average Christian feels this way, this is the reason they handle the Ten Commandments so lightly. We must not handle carelessly, these laws that God has given us. They were given not to be a hindrance, but given to help us live our lives with joy and happiness each and every day. The song writer states that "the longer I know him, the sweeter he grows", these commandments, help us to know our Heavenly Father in a more excellent way. It should be that all of us should desire to know him to the very best of our abilities. Another song states "to know, know, know him is to love, love, love him, and I do". Do you really, really know the Lord God Almighty; if you do, you will want to keep his precious Commandments.

4. "No other gods before me"

THE FIRST ONE IS "THOU shall not have any other gods before me". It is true that we are not seeing a lot of graven images like they had in what we call the ancient days. Folks still have graven images that they worship. It may not be something they made with their hands or it could be. Regardless if it occupies their time that they need to be spending with the God of creation, these false gods take up our worship time. You be the judge if your have other gods, standing between you and the eternal God, this would apply to whatever or wherever it may be. This would certainly qualify for having no other gods, before God. We deal with people's concept of what these Ten Laws represent. People in general feel that it's only sin if it is really bad in their eyes. The Prophet of old said "everyone did that which was right in his own eyes".

Concerning the Ten Commandments Jesus said, "If you have broken one of the least of these commandments you're guilty of all", is he trying to tell us how God looks upon all his commands. I'm not trying to make an excuse for the sins that causes folks to fall; I am trying to say that any Saint can fall through the breaking of any one of these commandments. I do not feel that the average Christian feels this way, this is the reason they handle the Ten Commandments so lightly. "No other gods before me", said the Lord; these other gods are in a literal sense, tearing the church of the Lord Jesus Christ apart. The devil is using their noncompliance to the Ten Commandments to destroy their lives and weaken the church as much as possible. Individuals need to have their eyes wide open, not seeing the value of this First commandment would seem to lessen the other nine. If this happens it will cause them to fall and fall hard. I do not think that most people willingly or perhaps I should have said, deliberately have other gods before

God, Satan, by his craftiness and subtlety leads men into all forms, of seeking after other gods. He whispers, ever so slightly and keeps on whispering in the ear ever quietly so he can lure the individual away from God. The great sadness is that this is multiplied to millions who are listening to the sound of his voice rather than giving attention to the commands of God.

5. "Thou shall make no graven images"

WE CREATE THROUGH OUR WORK, through our families, our recreation even our business practices, images that occupy and totally take our mind away from the living God. As a whole, people do not feel they are doing anything wrong. This leaves them without compassion regarding the fall of Saints, they would actually laugh me to scorn or anyone else, if they were told that what they are doing is just as wrong not in the eyes of men but in the eyes of God as one who steals. They would say you are crazy I am not guilty of any sin that would cast me down; you do not know what you are talking about. What I am trying to share is why we are as unforgiving as Christians. It is because most individuals feel that they are all right with God if they have not broken two or three of the worst of the Commandments. They in no way feel that the Commandments of God are all equal in the heart of God. If they are not equal why God did give us Ten Commandments to live by, I fully realize that the average person does not take into account the seriousness of keeping all of the Ten Commandments of God; therefore they are guilty of breaking according to Jesus all the commandments. What a twisted world we live in, a world where people listen to whispers of the Old Serpent. Instead of what God, Creator of all things has said. It was God, not man, that said do not create or make any thing that takes the place of your worship toward him. Folks who do so are headed for a mighty hard fall, a fall in which they are going to need help with. This means that every Christian that lives a committed life will have to be filled with compassion, caring, forgiveness, giving to others a hand up from the terrible fall that they have experienced. We are not out cutting a stump of wood and shaping it into the form of some animal or winged creature and then calling it our god. We do carve for ourselves many things in this life that we give so much allegiance to. These projects; they rob us and keep us from having a real good relationship with the God that created us. It is our duty and responsibility not to allow these kinds of things to happen in our lives. In regard to breaking God's commandments and this applies to all of them, one through ten. When we as individuals, break God's laws, we must understand it always starts in our hearts. We must do all we can keep our hearts in tune with God's will. Always remember "with the heart man believed unto righteousness and the mouth makes confession of sin" (ms). Remember God's word says, heart and mind, Satan tries to get into our mind, so he can destroy the work of God in our hearts, keep those Commandments. No idols of any kind will I allow in my life.

6. "Thou shall not take the name of the Lord thy God in vain"

I know that everyone views the Ten Commandments in different ways. There are sins of the flesh that are very serious, they destroy the goodness of man, his family, his friends and even the work that he may be trying to do. I do not know if you can put the Ten Commandments in chronological order, but they are listed starting with "no other gods before me",   God also said not to take my name in vain; we need to take a very close look at this third commandment. God said he would not hold anyone who used his name in profanity, innocent or guiltless. I understand this to mean that God holds man in a more serious way than what the average individual understands. Men and women, children and youth, folks of all age's, male, female are cursing using God's name in a very profane way. Even people that are active or what they would call active in their attendance at church, they also use God's name on a regular bases in a very profane way. These same people look down their noses at Christians who have fallen, theft, killing, sins of the flesh, adultery. Remember there is not any sin that God can not forgive except one, "blaspheming the Holy Spirit". This blaspheming is rejection of Jesus Christ as Savior. Indeed this is a terrible sin; we in society will have to deal with this sin everyday. The question I ask, are the Laws mentioned worse than the other commandments. I know that there are three commandments that affect society more than the others, I still have a lingering desire to know if God looks on these sins the way we do, or could it be that all the commandments of God are co-equal with each other in the heart of God. God tells us in his word that the tongue cannot be ruled, it is an evil not easily controlled, and tells us it cannot be tamed. Men on the earth allow all manner of evil to pour out of their mouths. The worst of these evils is when men use the Lord God's name in vain, and the word of God tells us "that he will not hold them guiltless who take his name in vain" (ms). We must be very careful with things we allow our minds to entertain, that is be careful what you think, it will pour out of your mouth. What comes out of our mouth must not be dishonoring to our God. In society, we have departed from the way God wants us to live; we hear all manner of cursing and profanity from people, almost any place that you go. And this includes children and our youth. We are becoming a nation whose mouth is filled with garbage of corruption, and it must not be so. We can change the way we speak, the way we use God's name in vulgar ways. If we will only turn and give heed to those commandments of God, given to help us live the best life possible.

7. "Remember the Sabbath day and keep it Holy"

THIS IS THE FOURTH COMMANDMENT that God gave to Moses on Mount Sinai. Are we to imagine that God was not serious about this, His, special day. It seems that maybe we are not serious about this day as we should be, evidenced by the way people live and conduct their affairs. The Largest portion of the quote, unquote Christians cannot be found on any given Sunday in Gods house. This leads me to believe that they do not take serious the fourth commandment; their heart would be torn if they truly understood the importance of Gods Day. The way they live and conduct themselves it appears that they are saying that reverence to God is not important. They will condemn the sins of the flesh; it seems evident, that it is all right not to honor God's day. Is God's heart broken because of the way people are living, not giving heed to what the commandments say concerning God's day? Do you suppose that God is taking very serious notice of their conduct? As an individual, if as Jesus stated, you break any of these commandments you are guilty, of breaking all His laws. We are in a terrible mess if we break one, give earnest heed to how we stand guilty of breaking all. I think we are in a lot more danger than we want to accept, what an awful mess we find ourselves guilty of. By taking a close look at the Ten Commandments we can begin to understand if we have an open heart what kind of sins we are committing against a Holy God. We may feel that we are totally safe from these first Commandments, surely we will be okay with this next commandment. Most people on the earth do not reverence Gods day, they are all busy doing anything and everything except being in the house of God and worshiping his precious name. Men should give the best of their lives by worship of the Christ of God. God tells us in his word that we have six days to take care of all of our labors, but the seventh day is holy unto the Lord. Not remembering Gods day they literally shows the self-centeredness and arrogance of men on the earth. It seems that man has time to do everything he wants to do, but he has no time for worshiping and praising the one who created and made him and gave to him a soul. God promise to us is if we love him. We shall live with him in the place of heaven for all eternity. Worship is important to God, and it should be important to you. If you have not been taking time to attend a church and give praise to him that made you, it is past time for you to take time and remember God's day. The best gift you can give to your children, family, friends and neighbors, is for you to be the best example possible showing them the way. God expects men to live here on this earth. I ask you this question, is there anything in your life that you reverence and keep holy? If there is not there certainly should be, first and foremost it should be God. If it is not God, then what comes first in your life? He gave to us the best, very best of heaven that you and I could have our sins forgiven, providing for us in place in his kingdom for all time. We must have our priorities in order, there is a reason why God gave unto us laws to help us to have the best life possible. He did not give us thousands or hundreds of laws; he made it simple for us if we would just obey them, just Ten Commandments.

8. "Honor thy father and my mother"

IF WE WERE TO TAKE an honest examination of our lives from the time we were very young until now, could we say we have kept this law of God. Would you say that you have always honored your father and mother? I will give you an example, there are two or three in the church were I serve at this very hour; they are dishonoring either their father or their mother. They consciously break the heart of one of their parents through their dishonor of this law. I do not feel that they think they are dishonoring their parents, they may look at themselves in the mirror and think everything is all right, they are looking in the wrong place, they need to be looking up to see if they are dishonoring God or not. Again is this commandment co-equal with the other nine Commandments? To answer the question, I believe if you break this commandment you are dishonoring God in your life. Men, women and children, blatantly dishonor their parents every day. It breaks my heart to see the way parents allow their children to treat them and speak to them. In many cases, I feel like they should be carried out to the woodshed, where they can have a conversation with a willow switch. I realize we have those in our society that always want to holler Child abuse, what about the parent abuse. Children speak evil of their parents and treat them very awful ways. With this going on in the homes it spills over into the schools, playgrounds, shopping malls, theaters, ballgames, anywhere that young people meet, they dishonor their parents with talk and the things they say. They dishonor their parents by the way they live, their involvement with liquor, drugs, pornography, and their blatant disrespect for law. They live immoral and indecent lives thus they dishonor themselves as well as their parents. Children dishonor their parents when they get too old to take care of themselves, they are placed in what we call "old folks homes", I know they have nicer sounding names for them today, but that is still what they are. Sometimes it is necessary for health reasons for person to be placed in the senior care facility, we understand this. We do not understand children placing their parents in places like this and for all practical purposes, they never come back and check on them, they just leave them there all alone as if they are not important anymore. These are the ones that brought children into the world and cared for them and nourished them through all their younger days when they could not care for themselves. Now their children dishonor them by not showing love, concern, as well as compassion. With this law breaking attitude, God is not well pleased and will hold all such accountable.

9. "Thou shall not kill"

THIS WOULD SEEM ON THE surface to be a commandment of God that would be the easiest of all them, the easiest for us on the earth to keep. Everyday on the news we hear reports of one individual killing another individual. The book of Genesis records for us what God said to Cain "the blood of Abel thy brother cries to me from the ground", ever since that day man has been killing man. Many times a person takes another life over what amounts to nothing, no just cause at all, our prisons are overflowing with convicts who have taken someone else's life. It seems that the life which God tells us about is very valuable, so valuable that he gave to each one of us a soul that will never die. The larger percentage of the population of the world will never kill another individual; that being said, there is still a lot of killing on the earth. We have killings in times of war, God's word tells us about war and what will happen during war, this kind of killing has to be different than what we see in the newspapers and on television each and everyday. A very large percentage of our television entertainment involves the killing of people, most of the time it is of innocent individuals; in many cases it is the killing of young children. We know that God will hold those that do the killing to accountability. What about the millions that have been killed through Abortion, we as a nation have endorsed, this kind of killing. David said "even before I was conceived in my mother's womb, you knew me" (ms). David is talking about God. I wonder how God looks upon society that has the ability to put to a stop to a large percentage of the killings that takes place if we had more honest judges, lawyers, district attorneys, our legal system is corrupt to a large degree. If a man knew he was going to give his life for the taking of a life. I believe that killings would go down; most killers know that if they are found guilty in all likelihood it will be at least eighteen to twenty years before the death sentence will take place, or better yet get out of prison in twelve to fifteen years on parole. With this in mind it is not difficult for me to say that this is not justice, and certainly not in keeping with the Ten Commandments of God, thou shall not kill. I give to you an example of the law being corrupt. A man owns a store and is robbed at the point of a gun. A man is robbed and killed who owns a store. In most cases the man who committed the armed robbery will spend more time in prison than the man who committed murder. How is that justice? God's Word tells how those who kill are to be treated. Worst of all murder is premeditation to take away the life of another. God understands human nature knows the trials that we endure in this life, he knows our limitations. There is such a thing as manslaughter, and God took this into account when he told our ancient fathers how to deal with each situation. God knows that others lives can be taken without intent and that man should be judged accordingly. Every time you look at any kind of news media, it will be revealed to you, how different individuals have died in the last few hours. I am not talking about natural deaths, but how individuals have been killed by others. They became angry for the most part, over things of very little value, yet they took someone else's life. God gave us these precious Commandments to help us live honestly and courteously each and every day. Murder would cease if we would only abide by one simple statement "do unto others as you would have them do unto you". If we follow his Commandments we will have a much better society to live our lives in. God knew all about us. That's why he gave us these laws.

10. "Thou shall not commit adultery"

THIS COMMANDMENT OF GOD IS broken every day, in every city, state, community; it is a sin that is running rampant like a wild disease over the length and breadth of this land that we love. In many cases a date with the opposite sex implies having sexual activities with each other before the evening is over. Young people, people of all ages are involved in adultery; they live together as if they are doing nothing wrong. In the good old days we called it "shacking up"; when I was a boy society would not tolerate this kind of living, in this day and time a large percentage of the population seem to feel that it's all right. It used to be in someone else's town or at least in far a way place but now it can be next door. People even come to church, and they need to be in church, but they should not be living together when they are not married. They act as if it is all right, but God will bring this into judgment. I feel that he will unless, that person does ask God to forgive them of their sins of adultery, and do it no more. We are still left with the consequence of sin to deal with. Society views the sins of the flesh more serious with God than all the other nine put together. If they are co-equal with God, will God judge all the sins of those who break the Ten Commandments? If David as King was guilty of adultery and the Bible tell us that he was guilty of this sin. The sin of adultery and the consequences of his actions caused him to loose the life of his young son. That is why David cried out "against God and God only have I committed this great sin" (ms). There is no doubt that adultery is a terrible act against God, it destroys lives, it destroys homes, it destroys families, it destroys business, it can tare a church apart, and lives can be ruined forever. Adultery is ugly and will be judged by the Lord God who gave us the Ten Commandments to live by. Adultery leaves a scar upon a life for as long as a person lives on this earth. Adultery is not just a single act, but rather, it is something that will do damage to the individual for the rest of his or her life. A statement is made here that you need to understand, we have become a people who like to use the term "the devil made me do it". Satan cannot make you do anything he can whisper his sweet lies in your ear to make even adultery seem to be all right. We do not like to be demeaning to other individuals, sometimes we need to simply understand the way that it is and what it does to us. I am speaking of this sin of the flesh, this thing we call adultery. When we break God's law we are drawn away by our lust, it is true that Satan can tempt you but he cannot make you sin. It is the lust in our hearts that causes us to break this law of God and it starts deep down in our hearts. What I am about to say might sound bad but it only describes the reality of those who commit adultery. Men and women in this situation are like two dogs in heat. This is the way they act and behave, craving with sexual appetite toward each other, when the act is over it may happen again or it may not. In many cases, it will continue, because it's deep-rooted in the heart of individual. In other lives it may stop because the individual feels the hurt and pain of what the lust has done to their life. God knew what lust would do to the human heart, so he gave us this Commandment not depriving us, but rather helping us to live the best life possible. Having said all this it will do us no good unless we obey the laws of God.

11. "Thou shall not steal"

WE AS A SOCIETY OF Christians turn our backs on those who steal. Yet it is quite evident that Christians steal, I do not know how large a percentage this would be. It is totally evident that Christians steal from God all the time. "Bring you all the tithes into the storehouse of the Lord" (ms), God Commands that ten per cent of what we earn belongs to him. Individuals do not understand that God is a good collector, people find themselves stealing from God on a regular basis and they think nothing of it. We are real condemning toward other people who have broken one of the other Ten Commandments. Again is this commandment: co-equal with the other nine commandments, do you feel that God thinks it is all right if you steal from him. You may not be breaking this Holy Law but you are very angry and upset against those that do break this law. If you found someone that said they were your friend or someone who said they loved you, if they stole from you, what would your feeling's be? You would call them a thief, and you would be right to call a person such a name. I wonder if God thinks you are a thief because you steal from him. I think he will hold all that steal from him, those who break his commandments. God will hold them accountable on the great day that is coming. It is not a sin that will send you to prison but it might be a sin that keeps you out of Heaven. God is the one who said; "if you love me keep my commandments". My wife works for a large retail operation, and I am just amazed when she tells me of what people are stealing and this goes on all over the country. Millions and millions of dollars of merchandise are stolen each day, they still little items that they put in their pockets, or there are many brazen thieves that steal very large items. Items like air conditioning units, riding lawn mowers, television sets, computers, chainsaws and the like. It takes a lot of nerve to take one of these big items and just walk out of the store with it, hoping that no one will stop them, and many, many times they are not caught. The moral fiber of so many people is to take what is not theirs, they use the excuse, it will not hurt them, and they can afford the loss. Many people make stealing a way of life and our prisons have been enlarged, because of the breaking of this Commandment concerning stealing.

12. "Thou shall not bear false witness against thy neighbor"

THIS IS A COMMANDMENT THAT many feel like they are never guilty of. We have to be extremely careful that what we say regarding our neighbors is always true. If we say slanderous things against our neighbors, things that are not true, we can do a lot of damage to their lives. Sometimes we as human beings get angry and upset at our neighbors; we say things trying to hurt them. Jesus said "love thy neighbor as thyself"; it is a hard job to love someone else like you love yourself. Jesus thought it important that every day; we should do our best to treat our neighbors as we ourselves would like to be treated. If our neighbors have done something terribly wrong we should take it to the proper author-ities. It seems like most of the time we try to take care of it ourselves. This is where we get into problems slamming our neighbors by saying untruthful things against them. We need to always try to put ourselves in the po-sition that our neighbors are in, always trying to say the right things and do the right things in regard to our neighbors. The old saying "do not judge another until you have walked a mile in his shoes", this is very good advice, do not be one who bares false witness. I have in my lifetime come to understand what Benja-min Franklin said so many years ago "I have so many times thought I was so right to find out that I was so wrong, that I have become very tolerant of other people's views". We can easily bare false witness, remember that this is a commandment of God. God will hold us accountable for how we have dealt with our neighbors during our lifetime. We must practice the old saying "do unto others as you would have them do and you". God put this Commandment in place for us because he knew with our human emotions and human ideas how easily it would be for us to bare false witness against our neighbor's. We have trouble with our emotional feelings therefore, it becomes easy with Satan whispering in our ear to do this or do that, to be false in our attitude toward our neighbors. None of us like to be mistreated therefore we should not mistreat others.

A pastor friend of mine recently had some people in his church to bear false witness against him. Understand with me that there are many ways to bare false witness. In his case two deacons ask him to meet with them because they had problems in the church. In his phone conversation with the one that called him. He was led to believe that they have some real serious problems that must be addressed. The area, missionary, was also invited to this meeting, when the meeting started the pastor asked what the problems were. He was told that everyone, (when you use this word it implies every person in the church) was dissatisfied with the way he was conducting himself. The first accusation was that he preached too loud, he does preach loud and has been doing so for forty five years without compliant. Next accusation was that he referred to his writing of spiritual materials to often while he was preaching. The third accusation was that he preached down to them, whatever that means. They continued with three or four other items that amounted to nothing. The accusations were so insignificant that even the missionary told the men that what they were doing was utterly ridiculous. Nonetheless, they stated that the people of the congregation did not want him behind the pulpit ever again. What they had done was to bring false witness against another individual. Considering the phone calls the pastor received during the next week it was evident that a great number of the congregation had no knowledge of what these men were talking about. The pastor having no desire to hurt anyone in the church agreed to resign and not be there on Sunday. Adding to bearing false witness they took away a great deal of his livelihood, leaving him in a position where he could not pay his house note or the note on his transportation. From this you can see the great harm. When a false witness is born against a person it can create tremendous, hard and difficult times for the individual who has been falsely torn down. This is the reason why God in his Commandments list certain concepts and ideas that we are to pay close attention to, so that society can live side-by-side without these kinds of problems and difficulties. We need to give more heed to what God deliberately has given, to keep us from such harm.

13. "Thou shall not covet anything that is thy Neighbors"

THIS IS THE LAST OF the Ten Commandments but it may not be the least of the Ten Commandments, this you have to judge for yourself. To covet is to want what someone else has; homes, boat, car, swimming pool, money, leisure time. The Bible states "not his servant, nor his maid, his ass, his wife, not anything that is thy neighbors" (ms). You might think it is the least, by saying why would anyone want what his neighbors has, the devil might lull you to sleep and before you know it you might want what is your neighbor. Boy that is a beautiful car, wish I had a swimming pool, if only I had the kind of money he has, what I am trying to tell you, unbeknown to you on a conscious level you might begin to want what your neighbor has. Be very careful, it is here that this commandment might link to another command, here is how it works. My neighbor's wife is very beautiful; making a mental acknowledgment of her beauty is not wrong, but day after day as you look upon her. Before you know it you want her, you wonder what she would be like in your bed. You did not intend to think like this it just happened or it least that is what you tell yourself. That is why it so very important not to covet what your neighbor has. To covet, will wind up in sin, and that sin can cause you to dishonor yourself, dishonor your neighbor and dishonor most of all the True and Living God.

God gave us these commandments so that we can live at peace with him and with our fellow man. Do not be guilty of breaking these Ten Commandments, if you do you will join the company of Saints who have fallen or if you are not a Christian to break these commandments will send you straight to hell. You might tell yourself I do not agree with you, I do not believe the Bible is true, many will follow this path, this will not change anything, the Bible tells us "the soul that Sins shall die", if you wish to run the risk of losing your soul it is your choice, God help you! I have a longing in my heart to know how serious these Ten Commandments are. I want you to have a good understanding of how important these Commandments really are to you. If you place the Commandments beside other scriptures like "all liars", now this is not included in the Ten Commandments but I beg of you let your heart and your mind comprehend how serious these ten laws of God are to you. The reason Saints fall is that they quit thinking of the laws of God, God did not give us but Ten Commandments, and I feel we are not trying to live by them. Some Saints will be restored, some never get up from the fall, Satan has them in his talons of ruin, while others are not Saints they are just folks who are lost, who one day soon they will meet their "Waterloo". Jesus said "all liars shall have their part in the lake of fire", that being true what happens with the unregenerate individuals who break and pay no attention to the commandments of God. I will leave this with you to see if you need to make some changes in your life concerning the Lord Jesus Christ. In Revelations it tells us that "the unbelieving, shall be cast into the lake of fire". We must hear what the Ten Commandments of God are saying to us! They give us life and happiness while we travel through this Earth.

Jehovah, the Holy One gave us the commandments as a goal, to know how to live for God. How we also should live socially. The question comes up can these ten laws of God give to us salvation? Sure they could if they were all ten completely kept everyday of our lives. We know this is impossible and this is the reason God gave us a perfect sacrifice of heaven Prince, our Savior, the Lord Jesus Christ. As we have already determined in the first of this writing Jesus put great emphasis on these Ten Commandments of God. How important they were to God as well as how important they are to us, to be kept. Each one of them bears a truth that God wanted us to live by. And we must obey what these laws are saying to us. God wrote these laws to be strong for man. Important I would say absolutely so. God wrote the law's to be as if they were written "on fleshly tables of the heart". When we as individuals begin to desire, what our neighbor has, that is what coveting means, we become in direct violation of this Commandment that God's has given to us. Our neighbors and friends have the things they have, because they work for them in order to acquire them. And we must never lust after anything that is our neighbors, including persons, as well as possessions. What if everyone was constantly coveting anything you might imagine that is your neighbor's, it would not take long for this sin to create such a commotion among society, that we would have a hard time to have decency and order that we might carry on our lives. God knew full well our weaknesses so he gave us laws to govern us that we might not fall into some awful disorder, and then disaster. Work hard, achieve, use what you have obtained for your benefit, but do not be envious or covet what your neighbor has. This law is a principal laid down for us to have the best life possible here on this earth. This law of God was given for our benefits, and our happiness, obey it faithfully!

14. In our best Interest!

MANY TIMES IN LIFE AS we busy ourselves with things that is in our best interest. We forget that God has always done everything in regard to us, for our best interest. This is the primary reason that God gave to us the Ten Commandments. These laws of God are in our best interest to provide for us the best quality of life that we can have on this earth. We live our lives as if these laws are not that important, Israel also did the very same thing in the very beginning of becoming a nation. The apostle Paul writes in the book of Corinthians in the 10th chapter. He reveals some very important things showing us, we need to follow the laws of God. As he writes to the church at Corinth he is trying to get the

Corinthians to understand what God did for the Jews in their beginning. He first spoke; they should not be ignorant of the things that happen in the past. He states that {all} of the fathers in those early days as they are coming out of bondage, were under the cloud of God's divine protection. He then states that {all} Passed through the Red Sea. He is reiterating that none were left behind, and God's great love for his people was shown by his parting of the Red Sea. If God is going to give to his people this kind of guidance, we should be desirous to keep his laws that he has given us. He also states that {all} were baptized unto Moses, this by showing a path through the Red Sea and the cloud to protect them by day, as well as the pillar of fire by night. He then hurriedly shares that {all} did eat of the same spiritual meat. To this he adds that they {all} drank of the same spiritual drink, he is not talking about the water that gushed from the rock, rather he is talking about the spiritual rock that followed them. And that rock is the Lord Jesus Christ. One of the promises that Jesus gave us, that faith in him would create wells of living water coming up from the inside wherein we would never thirst again. The word {all} is used five times in the opening part of this tenth chapter. Paul is emphasizing to this young nation that all were participants of God's blessings and God's deliverance. Therefore we who are saved have become by the grafting process the new nation of Israel, {all} of the deliverances that God gave to Israel he also will give to us. Because God takes care of us in this fashion we should obey his commandments, he tells us his commandments are not a hard to obey. What God does is always in our best interest, unless we have totally rebelled against him. God expects us to pursue happiness, and the closer we follow the laws that he has given us, we will be in pursuit for what is best for us, and accomplished by us. All God ever has wanted for us, is for us to love him with all our hearts and be very best person that he will help us to be by his grace.

15. Our best interest does not concern us!

I HAVE NEVER UNDERSTOOD WHY we on the earth are not concerned for what is in our best interest. We busy ourselves following, after things that do harm to our living each and every day. In this book of Corinthians, Paul shares with us, with many of the Israelites God was not well pleased. God certainly did not say all of the Israelites, but with many of them. He was not well pleased. This is the reason that those above twenty years of age died in the wilderness journey of forty years. This young nation had disobeyed God's command. They were hard hearted, stiff necked, they had rebellious hearts and they would not follow what God had told them to do. We are constantly looking at people, just like us, who are not heeding the commandments of God. Many think because the things we have been sharing are from the Old Testament that we in this New Testament day are not responsible to keep the commandments of God. But we are just as accountable to keep the commandments of God, as was Israel in her day, even to the present day. The Bible tells us in a way of a reminder that these, as God expresses {all} were participants in the blessings and many God was not well pleased with. He also tells us that these are examples to us, showing us the importance of keeping God's law. We should not lust after things of this world, as Israel lusted to their own hurt. They worshiped idols, do we worship idols? The truth is, we do, and idol is anything in our lives that we put before our worship and service to God. As God told them not to be idolaters, the same holds true for us today. It is said of Israel, while Moses was in the mountain receiving these commandments from God, that Israel began to behave in a riotous way, committing fornication, drinking intoxicating drink, the words used were "they rose up to play". They convinced Aaron to build them a golden calf, having done so, they worshiped this idol. When Moses came down from the mount, seeing what the Israelites were doing, he broke the tables of stone on which God had written Ten Commandments that he expected his people to live in obedience to them. On that day because of their forsaking the laws of God he destroyed them. On that day twenty three thousand died what a waste that was caused by disobedience to God's laws. Paul adds that we should not tempt God, by disobeying his laws as Israel did, for their disobedience, a plague of serpents was sent among them. They complained and murmured and were destroyed by the destroyer. This all happened by their willful disallowing God's law. If it could happen to them, what makes us think today that something terrible will not happen to us? We have become a people that have been given so much through prosperity that many live, work and act as if God is not concerned about the things we do, places we go and the people that we associate with. It seems that we are not concerned about what is best for us, just give us what we want, we are living a lot like the song that states "I swear there is not a heaven and pray there is not a hell". This implies to me with this kind of attitude that we are not concerned about what is best for us. As a songwriter saying, no hell, no heaven, when we die that is all there is. Evidently a lot of people feel this way; this is evidenced by the way people live today. The greater part of the population of this earth does not seem to be concerned about the things that should be the most important to them. They are not concerned about God or their fellow man, it is incredible but true folks are not concerned about what is in their best interest, what will benefit them the most in this life. The laws of God were designed for us to follow them in order to have the best life possible. Turn your attention to the Ten Commandments of God and strive to keep them for they will bring joy and peace to your heart, Amen!

16. The purpose for there example!

PAUL STATES THAT FOR US that live in the end days, these things are for our example. And they have been left for us for our instruction. Many would say instruction in what, instruction for us to learn to keep God's law, yes God's law. That which he gave to Moses on the mountain are sacred laws, and we should do our best to keep these laws to live at peace with God, also live at peace with our fellow men. We have to be very careful in trying to stand in our own strength. We are subject to fall at anytime, for strength does not come from man, our strength comes from the living God and we need to reverence him. We will be tempted, but with temptation we can overcome if we are walking within the confines of God's law. A lot of things may afflict us, but we can overcome these things, by and through the Lord Jesus Christ our Savior and Redeemer. God has given to us. His Ten Commandments to make our lives better, they were not given, to be a burden to us. If we get honest with ourselves, the burden comes when we allow Satan to deceive us, by whispering into our ear, that these commandments are not that important. How important are these commandments to you? I hope and it is my prayer that they are very, very important to you and your family and also to your friends. Jesus shared with us that we are to love the Lord with all our hearts and all our minds and with all our strength and to love our neighbors as ourselves. These two things will help us faithfully keep God's laws. If all of us would keep God's law, what a difference it would make in the world in which we live. God has a purpose in everything he does and these laws are part of that purpose, they will bless us for good and keep us from harm. Remember that God wrote with his own finger these laws on the tablets of stone for us to be the best that is possible for us to be. All of us should want the best for ourselves, our family, our friends and all of our relations. These laws would help us to have the best if we keep them. I must add the only true way to be the best you can be is to receive Jesus Christ as your personal savior and believe on him. In honoring Jesus, we honor God, the one who created us from the dust of the earth and breathed into us the breath of life and we became a living soul. It is God's desire that we take excellent care of our souls, which will always exist either in heaven in light or the lake of fire, where Satan lives. The choice of where you spend all eternity is your choice. You must receive Jesus or reject him, then he will write your name in the book of life certifying you will live with him forever, to deny him is to spend eternity in separation from him. You must decide and I certainly hope that your decision is the right decision. The odds are beginning to mount against society, because of their wickedness in the sin she continues to commit willfully with arrogance and pride. Please look again at the Ten Commandments and realize the way God intended for us to live, to be more personal, for you to live.

17. Becoming a Castaway!

IN DISOBEYING GOD WE BECOME castaways. We become, like individuals who have just drifted and drifted farther and farther away from where we are supposed to be, just a castaway. Castaways can be found and brought back where they need to be, but when individuals disobey God's laws it makes it very difficult in most cases, to bring them back to a safe harbor. The word is castaway, and not cast-offs, many people, by the way they live and conduct themselves they will be with time just cast-offs. It's a terrible thing to be a castaway, but far worse to be cast-offs. The best way for a castaway to get back home, to the place where they belong, is to keep the commandments of God. I do not think I could repeat it often enough to share the importance for all of us to keep God's commandments. If as Solomon stated "here the conclusion of the whole matter, fear God and keep his commandments for this is the whole duty of man". I encourage you to keep these laws of God that you do not become a castaway. More than that, you will not become cast-offs. Because you are being and not doing God's will for your life. I feel that God is as serious as possible when he gave them to us. These commandments from Mount Sinai were given to guide us through life. There is the Mosaic Law, the things to do and the things not to do. These are given for all occasions to guide and protect man in any situation that might occur in a society of men. But these Ten Commandments are much different from the Mosaic laws, they were written down by men with the leadership of God. But these laws from Sinai were written with the finger of God. Do not be a castaway, which could lead you to be cast-offs; this could break all fellowship between you and God as well as with other men. We should sincerely desire, not just put up signs in your front yard about these laws of God. Rather we should take these Ten Commandments of God very seriously and use them as a guide for us as we live our lives day by day. If we tried our best to keep them our prisons would become empty, very little need for police protection, our schools and communities would be safe havens for our children, security companies would go out of business, there would be no hard feelings among neighbors, divorce would be a thing of the past, no loss of life at the hand of another, our churches would be overflowed with people, Our pass time on Sunday, would be worship of Jesus Christ, no hard feeling between parents and children, no use of liquor, no drugs, no obscenities, no adultery, satisfaction with what you have, no child molesters, no crimes, no rape's or any other criminal activity. You would not have to lock your home or car and in reality not even your business. Think how wonderful it would be to live like that, if we would keep God's Ten Commandments we could live like that, no castaways or cast-offs, just living in the light of God's holy and precious word. The reason God gave us his laws was to give us the opportunity to have this kind of life. Even though many persons around you are not trying to keep God's laws, is no excuse for you and I not to do our best to keep the

Ten Commandments of God. Castaways are all around us, because of their rejection of God's means of living for Him. Others are just cast-off, what a pity to be cast-off in the Lord Jesus Christ. On the other hand, the castaways like the prodigal son did, they can repent of their sins and find their way back home again. There is always great rejoicing when one has wandered away, returned back safely, where God intends for them to be. I now ask you the question, are you were God intends for you to be, if the answer is yes (That's marvelous). If the answer is no that is a great tragedy. The Commandments will help guide you and Jesus Christ will save you. Is God's serious about these commandments? The answer is, you bet your life, God is very serious about the law He set down to guide men through this world.

18. The loss it brings!

I REALLY BELIEVE WE ARE in great danger of losing our nation, the land of our nativity if the church of Jesus Christ does not stand up and become the leaders of this land that God gave to us. We have not kept his laws and we have convinced ourselves that they are not important for us to live by. They are important for us to put them on our walls, plaques, monuments but most important keep them with all our heart. We must use them as a standard that reveals to us and to others how we are to live under God's glory.

Each of these laws or commandments are unique to help each of us have the needs in our lives met. We are to honor God in regard to what he has given us to have for our guidance, and the path he wants us to walk in. I must say again these are not suggestions, but Commandments. There is a song I like that tells a great truth, it tells us--- "Jesus as you look below its worse now than then"--- referring to the time Jesus was here on the earth. That being true we are drawing near to the end? Sodom and the lands around her God destroyed because of their sinful way of living.

There is more fornication, adultery, homo-sexuality, perversion of every description today, than any time in the history of man. There's not a society on the earth that does not advocate end times. Our action or in-action toward God and his Ten Commandments, I believe are drawing us today to the very hour when God will say enough. The trumpet of God will sound and everything will change. Everyday our government is taking away our freedoms and our privileges, "we the people", seems to have no meaning and is being ignored just as we ignore God's love. Our leaders want to make us into a nation ruled by Washington and it seems they are trying to lead us into a one world government. If we abide by God's Ten Commandments the powers that be will crumble and fall. It is time to be and do what we say in who we are by "having no other gods before God" ms. It is late but not too late if we take a stand for Jesus Christ the Son of God our Savior and our Redeemer. Are you concerned about your nation in the direction in which she is taking? With an adherence to the laws of God, she can take the right direction and become truly "one nation under God, indivisible with liberty and justice for all". If ever there was a day that we need these laws of God, I believe it is today. God help us to become that people that you intended for us to be, and let us reverence you. In the beauty of the Holiness of God we will worship thee. It is not too late but we are ever getting closer to hearing "the Bell toll", when you hear it ringing you can be sure "it tolls for us". God is serious about these laws. It's time, let me add past time that these laws of God become very serious to us.

About the Author:

MELVIN SHARRY WAS BORN IN a small comminuty in Caddo County Oklahoma on January Eleventh, 1944. His family moved to Conroe, Texas when he was in the third grade. He spent his High School days at David Crockett High School. Later he attented East Texas Baptist College in Marshall, Texas for two years, then he took Seminary extension classes for two years. He then did a four year study with the Bible Institute in Alamo, Tennessee and received their Doctor of Divinity Degree in 1974. For 45 years he has served as pastor to churches in East Texas, North West La., also he served a mission church in Colorado. He makes his home with his wife Linda in Atlanta, Texas.